Rose

My Mother Was a Nun

GEMMA KEATLEY

BALBOA.
PRESS
A DIVISION OF HAY HOUSE

Balboa Press books may be ordered through booksellers or by contacting:

Balboa Press
A Division of Hay House
1663 Liberty Drive
Bloomington, IN 47403
www.balboapress.com.au
1 (877) 407-4847

Because of the dynamic nature of the Internet, any web addresses or links contained in this book may have changed since publication and may no longer be valid. The views expressed in this work are solely those of the author and do not necessarily reflect the views of the publisher, and the publisher hereby disclaims any responsibility for them.

The author of this book does not dispense medical advice or prescribe the use of any technique as a form of treatment for physical, emotional, or medical problems without the advice of a physician, either directly or indirectly. The intent of the author is only to offer information of a general nature to help you in your quest for emotional and spiritual well-being. In the event you use any of the information in this book for yourself, which is your constitutional right, the author and the publisher assume no responsibility for your actions.

Any people depicted in stock imagery provided by Thinkstock are models, and such images are being used for illustrative purposes only.
Certain stock imagery © Thinkstock.

Printed in the United States of America.

ISBN: 978-1-4525-2439-9 (sc)
ISBN: 978-1-4525-2440-5 (e)

Balboa Press rev. date: 07/22/2014

Chapter 1

My name is Rose; I am seventeen years old. My mother was a nun; she was also my hero. When my mother was alive, I had no desire to know anything about my life. Everything I needed existed within her. She held my world together and gave me the only solid piece of love I ever experienced.

Now that my mother is gone, I can do nothing but search. I went to her old home, the place where she was born. I tended her garden. I spent time with the church minister who knew her, and I began to make sense of my life. This is my story.

I was born during the war. Well, the war had finished, but who knew the fighting continued? My birth mother was seventeen, and my father was twenty. When he was sixteen he lied about his age to fight for the country he loved, and that country destroyed him. He was one of the "lucky ones" who came home, but on most days, I think they both secretly wished he hadn't.

At night, my father would dream. He thought he was back in the war. He fought with my mother in his sleep, and he hurt her. He woke bathed in sweat, and he was sorry. During the day, he drank. He fought with my mother, and he beat her. This time he was not bathed in sweat, but he was still sorry.

When I was just a baby, I was crying. My tummy hurt, and I was hungry. My mum was lying on the floor and wouldn't get up. In her hand was an empty bottle of pills.

When my father found her, he flew into a rage. "I risked my life to save you, to save this whole country, and *this* is how you repay me?" He hit my mother in her unconscious state, and when I cried, he hit *me*. Again and again.

When he realised what he had done, he threw my limp and silent body into a rose bush in front of the vicarage and shot himself in the head with his service revolver.

Nice.

Chapter 2

The minister, a kind man, came out when he heard the gunshot. He didn't know what to do. He retrieved my body and was relieved to find I was still breathing. There was no hospital in the town, and medical help was in short supply. He cleaned me up as best he could, unsure of the extent of my internal injuries.

He fed me communion wine in the hopes it might numb the pain or ease my passing.

He performed the last rites as a precaution to protect my soul, all the while praying fervently to God to save me. He told me it is always God's will that we should pray for, but the war had taken so many innocent lives, he couldn't bear to lose yet another.

So, on that warm summer day, he sent for the police, to focus their efforts on the dead, so he could fully attend to the living.

I expected the police would take me, but I guess it was deemed the bastard child of a teenage mother was the jurisdiction of the clergy. As far as the minister was aware, I had no other living relative.

That very day, despite the fact that he would soon be ministering over two more funerals, he bundled me up and gathered some supplies, and together we rode on horseback for several days until we reached the abbey at the top of the hill.

*   *   *

As I sat in the vicarage seventeen years later, listening to him retell the story, I was confused as to why he would make such a long trek when surely there must have been an orphanage close by. I asked him about this, and his eyes took on a faraway look. "As God is my witness, I heard your mother call to me that day. When I heard the gunshot and I went out, I saw an apparition, she was right there in her habit and veil, standing over the rose bush, beckoning me to the abbey."

He spoke with such reverence and genuine belief that I didn't have the heart to tell him this was impossible. Instead, I smiled politely and took another sip of my tea.

Chapter 3

My mother kept a journal. It must have been important to her, as it was her only possession. She gave it to me just before she died. When I read it, it was as though she was talking directly to me. Did she know that one day I would inevitably be in possession of it, or did she just naturally express a lot of love through her writing?

I do not think I would have been so loving if I was writing a journal. In fact, I think I will try it and see what comes out for me. My mother had such wisdom and compassion, whereas I just see life as it is: unfair.

If you asked me what is important in life, I would not say *love* or *education* or *time*. For me, it is not material success or admiration. I believe the most important thing in life is connection. Not with everyone, or even most people, but a real, genuine, loving connection with your special someone. For me, it wasn't my birth mother, because I didn't have that opportunity. But my mum, well, she was different.

She stopped the world to be with me. She even interrupted her prayer time to kiss my head, hold my hand, or read to me. I don't know if she got into trouble for this or if God was mad that she picked me over prayer time, but these little things, these small acts of connection, impacted my life more deeply than she will ever know.

Reading her journal, I see now how much pressure she was under and how her life was neither easy nor straightforward. She had to fight for everything, and I think I forget this when I consider how easy she made life for me.

Chapter 4

*I*t's strange how the end of someone can be the beginning of someone else. My parents' passing was the beginning of a new life for my mother, as it brought me into her world; my mother's passing was the beginning of a new life for me, as I began to understand more of who I was and who I was to become.

This is not to say we should give up our lives in order to kick-start someone else's, but I know that in the end, when I left my job at the fishmongers, my farewell lunch was the most positive experience I had had during my time there.

I guess what I mean is that the biggest losses can lead to deep soul searching, but this doesn't have to be the only way.

Many times, after I was sent away from the abbey (and my mother) for work, I thought of ending my own life. I thought about all those around me who would finally realise how badly they had treated me, and how sorry they would be. I thought about the outpouring of grief, and eventually the appreciation of me, that in my fantasies would live on forever.

However, the reality of life is different.

Chapter 5

I think in life, we are looking for the grand gesture. We want to make a big sacrifice or a lifelong commitment to another person, and then we think we are done. But life is not about the big stuff; mostly life is about all of the little sacrifices.

Great people are made in the seconds of their lives, not in the hours. A gesture, a glance, putting your own life on hold to make a connection—well, these are the things that change the world.

It is the things we don't think too much about that make the biggest difference.

My mother did this for me, and I don't know what I gave her in return.

In her journal, she talks about me bringing so much joy, but truly I don't believe I ever brought her anything but trouble.

My arrival in the abbey caused no end of bitterness with the other sisters, and she could not start a new life because there I was, hanging around, being needy.

I'm sure she would say she saw it differently, but it makes me think. *How is it that we turn out the way we do?*

My birth mother was seventeen when she had me. Seventeen! I'm that age now, and sure, I feel like I own the world sometimes—but to have already had a baby who was totally dependent on me, and to be with someone like my dad, dealing with his own stuff? I'm not sure I would have done it differently than she did.

The women I knew in my life were strong. They got on with the task of living, and they did not complain. Me, I'm thinking of changing my middle name to Complain!

Surely I should just suck it up and be mature about it, but at the end of the day, I just want my mum. I just want to hear her voice and feel her touch. I just want to smell her hair and melt into her.

God was important to her, I guess, living in an abbey and all, but to me, God has some explaining to do.

I don't think I ever asked for too much. I didn't really know that my life could have been different, but now that I know it can be, I am furious. Furious that the world is actually not the safe, warm, happy place I imagined it would be.

I am determined to make my life better, but how do I survive without my special someone?

Chapter 6

When I was six years old I was sent down the hill from the abbey to the orphanage. At the time I thought I was so grown up. This was my opportunity to get out of the boring confines of the abbey and to finally have some adventure and some fun. In the beginning I loved the excitement of a new place to live, and other children to play with.

I was thrilled that I could sleep high up on a bunk bed in a room with ten or twelve other children. The bedroom was massive, and we were allowed to hang our arts and crafts on the walls. We each had a drawer to ourselves for our personal belongings, and I appreciated that I had my very own school clothes.

In the mornings we all ate together, and there was so much noise! In the abbey everyone was so stuffy and quiet. If I made a noise, everyone was crabby. Here there was laughter and clinking glasses, practical jokes and roughhousing. It was as though my eyes had been opened to the world.

When we brushed our teeth we would have a competition as to who could flick the most toothpaste on the mirror without getting caught. The person who got caught by the housemother had to clean it all off. It was my favourite game as I was very good at avoiding suspicion.

We used to spy on the housemothers as they knitted and sewed. They were so boring, but the spying was fun.

We spent our evenings playing truth or dare and sometimes a few of us would sneak into the kitchen to steal bread and jam. Usually just enough to not get caught.

There was always something going on.

I remember one day, one of the girls took another girl's hairbrush, and the fight was on. Both girls had handfuls of hair ripped out and black eyes, not to mention split lips and bruising from falling over each other as they rolled on the ground. At the time, it was the most shocking thing I had ever witnessed, yet it was so exhilarating.

What was even more shocking was the walloping they both received from the housemothers. Neither could sit down for a week. In some ways we felt sorry for them, but it didn't stop any of us from giving them a tap on the bottom when they went past us, or from waving our hairbrushes around, taunting, "Is this yours? Come and get it."

Looking back now, I know it was nasty, but it was a case of kill or be killed. There were those who were considered the top dogs. They were bossy and in charge. They were the practical jokers and the ones who determined who was to be picked on or who was to be left alone. If you wanted to make it here, you had to know how to play the game.

The boys were bad. They used to punch on with the other boys and tease the girls, but the girls were truly wicked.

One day the girls put bleach into my shampoo as a joke and turned my coppery red hair bright orange. The girls thought it was hilarious, and I got the beating for it, as the housemothers assumed I was giving myself a makeover.

The bruising was severe, but it was nothing compared to the humiliation of waiting for my hair to grow back. Chunks of it had begun to fall out, and what remained resembled straw.

I realised that if I was going to survive, I needed to make it to the top of the food chain. I began to hatch a plan.

Chapter 7

Our teacher was a frightening, nasty nun. We called her the Beast. She was angry all the time, and she walked around as if she owned the place (and us with it). She was ridiculously strict and hated me with a passion. If my nails were not clean enough she would strike my hands with a ruler. If I said my times tables too fast, or not clearly enough, I was sent to stand facing the wall. If I smiled, she would tell me to take the smirk off my face. She called me the Devil's child and said not even God himself would be willing to cleanse me of my sins.

I decided I needed to send a message to the other girls not to mess with me, and I would do this by messing with the biggest bully of all.

I let the other kids watch me as I put dirt in her coffee. They saw me hide her long whipping stick. They watched in horror as I scribbled in her daily roll book, and they froze in terror as I tore down the times tables chart that hung on the wall.

I knew I had gone too far, and a fear gripped my heart, but I couldn't undo what I had done, and everyone was watching. So, bravely I said to the other kids, "No one messes with me." I think they quite clearly got the point.

I still do not know how I survived the whipping I sustained when the Beast found her whipping stick. At the time I didn't know I had been beaten to within an inch of my life before by my father, but crudely, something about it did feel familiar.

I spent the next two days in the sick room, drifting in and out of consciousness. The housemothers had to send for the doctor to see if I would live. Even to this day my back is a scarred and ugly reminder of my desperate attempt to fit in with, and protect myself from, the other children.

I wore my injuries with pride. It was my badge of honour. The other children were in awe of me. The top dogs wanted me to be their friend, and the others, I think, were just plain scared of me.

I thought I was so strong and brave, and I was proud of myself for making a stand, until my mother came to visit. When I saw how she looked at me, with my bright-orange hair and battered body, I was so ashamed. I couldn't look at her, and I certainly couldn't embrace her, or explain myself.

I thought she would be furious with me, but she just cried and held me. As a six-year-old, I had no clue what she was thinking, but a few days later my mother came to take over teaching my class.

The other children thought this was brilliant. Finally someone kind and gentle who could teach us all we needed to know. I'm sure there were whispers about me being the favourite as she was my mother, but no one dared say a word to me. Everyone treated my mother with due respect— not only because she was wonderful, but, well, because my mother was under my protection.

Chapter 8

I t felt wonderful to be powerful and safe from the bullying of others. Now that I was at the top of the pecking order, I had no need to push anyone else around and I could focus better on my studies. I enjoyed learning new things and loved having the extra time to be with my mother. When new kids came into the orphanage, someone would always retell the story of Rose versus the Beast so my legend continued.

Being this person, however, made it difficult to truly connect with others. Life had become about survival more than anything else, and even though we all pretended that we were so close, I still felt different and completely isolated. I felt there was something wrong with me, and I didn't know how to fix it.

The other kids had a perception of me as being strong and powerful, someone to be respected and feared, and my mother had the perception that I was a wonderful, untarnished girl. Me, I couldn't work out who I was. I had such an isolated life and I knew so little of the world.

As I grew, I became incredibly bored by the monotony of my environment, my studies, and the people around me. I longed for adventure, for independence, for anything at all that was not this life.

My big break came on the eve of my thirteenth birthday. The housemothers had found me a job several villages away working for a fishmonger. This was my chance to escape.

I was obviously nervous about leaving my mother, and I knew I would miss her dreadfully, but this was my chance at a new life. I proudly cleaned out my drawer, which contained all my prized possessions. I took my hairbrush and handheld mirror, a photo of my mother, and a Bible my mother had given me when I was a child. For my birthday, my mother had given me a beautiful pen engraved with my name, as well as writing paper, envelopes, and stamps so we could continue to keep in touch.

My farewell was nothing fancy. Some of the kids from the orphanage had made me cards, and the housemothers gave me a stiff hug and wished me well. I couldn't help feeling they were all glad to be rid of me.

My mother cried and cried, and it took all my strength not to become a blubbering mess myself. I had learned over the last thirteen years of my life that it was much safer to hide your emotions, and I had had lots of practice, so I hugged her tightly, put on a stiff upper lip, and walked away, heart pounding, into a brave new world.

Chapter 9

My new village was incredible, a bustling hive of activity, right on the ocean. I had never seen the ocean before, and the vastness of the water was indescribable. The salty sea air invigorated me, and I knew something great was happening here.

The Baxters were my new employers. Mr. and Mrs. Baxter were well known in the fishing village. Mr. Baxter owned two fishing boats and had staff to run them, and he supplied seafood not only to the village but to neighbouring villages as well. His wife was a dressmaker and owned a local boutique.

Their home was like a castle. It was large and meticulously maintained. There were seven bedrooms, and each room was as large as a ballroom. The bathroom and the toilets were *inside* the house, a luxury I had never experienced before.

I was thrilled to learn the Baxters were to provide me with food and board, as well as a small wage. It was as if I had just been crowned a princess.

My bedroom was simply gorgeous. The curtains were a lovely cornflower blue with pale yellow and white flowers, and the bedspread was made from matching material. I had a large double wardrobe all to myself and a magnificent white dresser with a large mirror and a place to sit and brush my hair. My window let in an abundance of natural light and overlooked the ocean waves.

Lillian and Anne were also employed by the Baxters, and they were to be my housemates. Lillian, a beautiful fifteen-year-old girl was employed as a housemaid. She was responsible for taking care of the home and doing all the cooking. She made the most mouth-watering dishes, and she was very particular. She was always immaculately groomed and had the finest skin I had ever seen. Even her apron looked beautiful on her, and her nails were perfect. She was soft spoken, so it was difficult to get to know her. She had been employed by Mr. and Mrs. Baxter since she was thirteen, so I looked to her as a bit of a role model. She had a strange habit of touching all the doorknobs before she went to bed and locking and relocking doors at night, but I supposed we all have our quirks.

Anne was a large–framed, seventeen-year-old girl who was employed by Mrs. Baxter eighteen months ago. She was responsible for helping out in the dress shop. She was a bit more loudly spoken than Lillian and me, but she had a real kindness about her. I could tell by looking in her eyes that she'd had a hard life.

Together we shared this marvellous place, and though we did not get a chance to talk much, we each had a kindness and respect toward each other and an unspoken connection, a new experience for me.

My job was a bit dirtier than the other girls', and I lacked the airs and graces they had picked up during their employ. My job was to work on the wharf, cutting open the fish and cleaning them up for sale. It was dirty, smelly, messy work, but I loved the challenge of seeing how many fish I could clean, scale, and prepare each hour.

I loved the opportunity to be out in the fresh air, despite the fishy smell, and I enjoyed listening to the seagulls cawing as they hungrily devoured the scraps, and to see the happy people of this village go by.

In a very short space of time, I knew them all. I knew all the comings and goings, and I was a welcome sight in the village. Everyone would give me a wave and stop to say hello. They valued my opinion regarding what seafood would be best on their table for the evening, and I quickly became an integral part of Mr. Baxter's business.

Chapter 10

Mr. Baxter was a powerful man. He had a lot of wealth behind him and seemed to own half the village. He certainly worked very hard and seemed to be pleasant and likable. He was not an attractive man; he was short in stature and had a large belly and was slightly balding, but he had a certain charisma about him and seemed to know how to win people over. He was the first grown-up man I had come into contact with.

Mrs. Baxter was a lovely, large-built, and kind woman. She had ventured into dressmaking and sewing during the war in order to help the war effort and had spent a lot of time sewing parachutes, uniforms, and the like for the servicemen. For all I knew, she may have sewn my birth father's uniform.

After the war finished, she had opened up a boutique, and now that the economy was improving, she was making a great trade selling beautiful gowns and everyday wear to the ladies and gentlemen of the village.

I was thrilled, shortly after I arrived in the village, when Mrs. Baxter brought home some new clothes for me to wear, and offered to sew me some more herself. She knew just what colours would bring out my eyes, and which colours would complement my coppery red hair. My hair had long-since returned to normal after the bleaching incident, and it was lovely to have new clothes for the first time in my life.

I wrote to my mother all about it, and she replied that she was so very pleased to hear that life was working out so well for me. Life in the abbey continued on as normal as far as I was aware, so I was content to focus back on my new life.

Mr. and Mrs. Baxter never had any children of their own, and Mrs. Baxter once admitted this was because she was barren. I did not really have an education in how babies were made or what determined who could have them and who couldn't, so without any real understanding of what she was talking about, I just sympathised with her as best I could. She said there were worse things in life, and she had us girls now, so who could ask for more?

As Mr. and Mrs. Baxter were considered high society in the village, they often hosted dances that attracted all sorts of people from the nearby villages. As we were living with them, we were invited to attend these functions as guests. Lillian was generally still employed to serve during these occasions, but she had additional staff to help her, and she said she preferred to be invisible during these times.

Lillian's looks attracted a lot of attention from boys and men of all ages, and I think she felt uncomfortable about this. I had nothing to worry about, as no one was very interested in a redheaded fishmonger girl who spent each day wading through fish. Or so I thought.

Chapter 11

As it turns out, there was someone interested in me, and that was Mr. Baxter. Things started out very innocuously, with a comment here and there about what a beautiful young lady I was becoming, and brushing past me occasionally as I worked.

At first I thought this was just my imagination, but my gut said "danger." Mr. Baxter made excuses to check on my work during the day and would offer to tuck me in at night.

When Mrs. Baxter began working into the evenings over the summer with Anne, and Lillian had retired to the servants' quarters, Mr. Baxter would come into my bedroom. He would offer me sweets and help me to get into my nightdress. He always made out that this was a perfectly normal and natural thing to do and that it was part of taking care of me. He told me how pretty I was, and that the scars on my back were beautiful to him. He told me how soft my skin was. He told me he would like to touch my skin and that I could touch his if I wanted to.

I was in a panic and in a bind. I felt ill in my stomach and had no idea what to do. I was only thirteen. I knew nothing of these things and had no one to guide me. If this was normal and expected and I refused him, then he would be mad and I would be sent away. My mother would be ashamed of me, and then where would I end up?

So I let him touch me. I did as I was told, and I was so embarrassed and ashamed that I mentioned it to no one. The other girls never noticed, or if they did they never said anything. I don't know if I was the only one, or if he went to the others as well, but thinking about Lillian's penchant for locking doors and Anne's sad, troubled eyes, it would not have been out of the question.

I began to understand why Mr. Baxter had not employed a boy to be his fishmonger.

Chapter 12

The nighttime visits from Mr. Baxter continued regularly for several years. I dreaded the evenings as I never knew when the doorknob would turn.

As Mr. Baxter became more and more demanding in terms of what he expected me to do with him, I was overcome with a sense of helplessness and anxiety.

I began to drink. At first I just sneaked a sip here and there until gradually I increased my consumption, to the point where I couldn't go more than a few hours without a drink. Mrs. Baxter said nothing and did not seem to notice the bottles that went missing from her regular social gatherings. She was focussed on her business and left everything of importance to Lillian. Mr. Baxter would have surely smelt it on my breath, but to him it just served to make me all the more compliant.

Just shy of my sixteenth birthday I began to get my woman's cycle. I was completely shocked. I thought I had been broken, and I cried in fear, not knowing what was going on.

Lillian heard me crying and was a wonderful support. She explained what was happening and how to manage it. She told me I needed to be careful now. I asked her what she meant, and she just looked at me sadly and said it didn't matter; there was nothing I could do anyway.

I went through four cycles and then it stopped. I began filling out and felt ill all the time. Mr. Baxter first became angry and then worried. He took me to a specialist doctor from a neighbouring village.

I listened in confusion as he talked to the doctor about how a "young rascal from the village" must have "deflowered" his poor naive fish girl. The doctor shook his head and tut-tutted in sympathy with Mr. Baxter, and assured him he would take care of it swiftly, and with a minimum of fuss. He assured his utmost discretion in these sensitive circumstances.

With the formalities out of the way, Mr. Baxter handed the doctor a wad of cash and arranged to pick me up later that afternoon.

I was then exposed to the most painful, uncomfortable, and humiliating procedure, and the pieces of the puzzle began to fall into place.

The doctor chastised me for compromising Mr. Baxter's reputation. He said that at my age I should not be mixing with other boys and to let this be a lesson to me. He said he could not get rid of every baby that came along and that the only way for me to prevent this happening again was to avoid physical contact with the opposite sex.

My head was reeling. I had only just worked out how babies were made, and I had already lost one of my own. My heart shattered into a thousand pieces.

Chapter 13

Mr. Baxter was soothing and supportive. He told me how much he loved me and how proud he was of me for going through the procedure. He said I would always be his delicate flower, but he never came into my bedroom again.

For a time I waited anxiously and fearfully as usual, but as time went on I became confused. I had never wanted this man to touch me. I had never been attracted to him, and I had never done anything to lead him on, but there he had been the only man who had ever shown an interest in me. He was kind, and he desired me. He gave me a roof over my head, beautiful clothes and gifts, and a life I had only ever imagined.

I had grown accustomed to him, and now, just like that, he was gone. He treated me no differently during the day than he always had, but he would not look me in the eye. I began to believe I had let him down and convinced myself that maybe I loved him.

I was so ashamed of all these conflicting feelings, and I had no one to talk to about them. The drink was not helping, and neither were Mrs. Baxter's sleeping tablets and painkillers. So after much angst and deliberation, I did the unthinkable. I wrote to my mother.

I confessed everything. I prayed for her forgiveness, and I begged her for her wisdom and advice.

She never wrote back.

Chapter 14

At the time, I had no idea the Beast from my school days, who had been appointed the new Mother Superior, had been confiscating my letters. I did not realise my mother never read my confession and never received my plea for help. So a few months later, when I received word to come directly to the abbey because my mother was dying, I believed my letter had killed her.

I was reunited with my mother one last time, and all the troubles of my past melted away. My mother loved me, and that was all that mattered. My mother and I prayed together that God may grant us another lifetime together, and I wept.

I had lost my someone, and now I felt I was no one.

When I returned home to the Baxters, Mr. Baxter had employed another young girl with fair soft skin. She was barely twelve. I had been replaced, and I was devastated.

Chapter 15

My mother, the nun, her name was Mary. She was named after Mary of the Immaculate Conception. Funny, now I think about it, how I was my mother's immaculate conception.

Mary, our holy mother, had Jesus, the most important man who ever lived. He changed people's lives. He transformed them. He sacrificed himself and saved us all.

My mother had me. What a disappointment. Here I was, a nobody, and who would I save? Who would I help? Jesus sacrificed himself to cleanse the sins of man. It seemed to me that I was born into the world to reinstate them. I wanted to be good, and I wanted to bring good into the world, but I didn't know how.

Who would want to listen to a tale of a girl whom God himself had rejected? I had already lost two mothers and a father, and now even the man I had feared and despised for so long, Mr. Baxter, had rejected me as well.

I was lost and drowning. With the same level of hopelessness and despair that my birth mother must have felt, I took the lid from a bottle of painkillers, washed them down with a large glass of wine, and prayed for death to come swiftly.

Chapter 16

What actually happened was the turning point in my life. There were no angels or tunnels of light. My mother did not greet me with open arms, and I guess, more importantly, I did not fall into the devil's clutches.

What happened was that I vomited myself into a stupor. Seventeen years' worth of pain and anger and fear and bitterness spewed out onto the carpet. I was so violently ill that I genuinely thought I would die. Ironic, given that that's what I had initially intended to do.

And with this purging came a moment of complete clarity. I did not want to *die*. I wanted to live a life that I could be *proud* of. In that moment I realised I had not lost everything; *I* was still here, and *I* was the only one who could transform my life.

With this realisation came an incredible sense of freedom and power. I was responsible for me, and I could turn my life around.

Never had I been so enthusiastic or grateful about cleaning up my own mess.

Chapter 17

I made arrangements to leave the employ of the Baxters and travel back to the village where my mother was born. I had read her journal and had to find out more.

My farewell lunch was exquisite. Most of the village was there, and Mr. and Mrs. Baxter put on a lavish affair. There was music and dancing and the most beautiful speeches. I had never heard such glowing commendations from the local people, and Mrs. Baxter was genuinely tearful as she spoke of the blessing I had been to her. Lillian and Anne hugged me tightly for a long time, and we vowed to keep in touch.

Mr. Baxter said I was his best girl and that he would never forget me. He presented me with a large sum of money to help me on my way. Hush money or not, I accepted it graciously and left with a new sense of determination.

Chapter 18

I arrived in the village where my mother was born and went to her old home. I tended her memorial plot, were I placed an additional cross to represent her. The home was falling apart and in disrepair.

I took lodging above the general store using the money I had been given, and I made arrangements to speak with the minister who had found me.

The minister had a familiar warmth, as he told me what he knew of my mother and of me. I told him I intended to make a life for myself here in the village, and his eyes lit up with genuine excitement.

"I always knew God would call you home," he said, nodding in satisfaction.

"Well, I tried to go to God and he wouldn't take me, so I guess this is where he wants me to call home."

The minister got up and walked over to an old mahogany chest. He opened it carefully, his frail arms almost struggling under the weight of the lid. From it he took an old iron key. "Here," he said placing the key in my hands with both of his.

"What is it?"

"Your birthright." He said solemnly. When your mother, Mary, left here to become a nun, it was because she was grief-stricken, and she thought she had no other choice. She thought her life was over. She asked me to sell her family farm and to send half the takings to Mother Superior in the abbey, and keep half for my ministry. Well, I am a man of my word, and I did indeed send half of the value of the property to the abbey, but I decided to hold the rest of the estate in trust until its rightful heir returned to claim it."

"I knew it needed a lot of work and the others in the village questioned my sanity often over the years for keeping it, rather than turning it into profit, but somehow I knew that one day all would be set right, and that, *that* house would become a house of love and life again, rather than one of loss and sorrow."

"And now here you are, a vessel of much loss and sorrow yourself, waiting to be transformed with love and life."

I looked at the minister, my mouth hanging open in awe and surprise. Here was a man who valued me, understood me, and assisted me without any thought of personal gain. Here was a man who had waited for me, not knowing if I even existed, and held such hope for my redemption and resurrection. He was just like my mother, pure and decent and good.

Chapter 19

After speaking to the minister, I decided that up until now I had been living like I was a condemned building: damaged, falling apart, and just waiting to be demolished by life.

I had three choices. I could choose to die in the hopes that God would renew me, I could admit myself to an asylum and remain there for the rest of my days, or I could take charge of my life and rebuild myself from the ground up.

I figured my birth mother had already tried option number one and my mother had tried number two (the only difference being that her asylum was a house of God), so I went with option number three.

I decided that if I was going to rebuild myself, a full restoration was in order.

So I began to rebuild my new home, and with it myself.

As I cleared out my home and swept the place clean, I did the same with my body and my attitude.

In the past, alcohol had been my friend, my companion, and my crutch, but now that the restoration was in progress, I decided I needed to take charge. I began to water down my wine. That way, in the beginning, I could still drink as much as I was used to but it was having less effect. It tasted terrible but I guess that was the point.

I knew the threat of abuse was now gone, but my body did not believe me. So I decided to respect my body. This was a completely foreign concept to me, but hating myself was getting me nowhere, so I had to do something.

I began to eat well, good, tasty food in moderation. I began to feel grateful for the food that I put into my body and began to drink more water.

I got out into nature. I took deep breaths and enjoyed the fresh air again. I went walking a little every day, and I got my body into the water.

I rubbed soothing cream into my scars—not because they were sore, but to acknowledge that they were part of me, and that the pain of the past deserved to be soothed.

I took care with my appearance and stopped frowning at my hair every time I passed a mirror.

I began to make choices as though I intended to live.

Over time, I began relying less and less on alcohol to numb the pain, and finally I was able to let the addiction go.

Chapter 20

I asked around the village for work, and it seemed my mother's God was smiling upon me after all, as I was taken on as an apprentice by the village baker. I worked from 5:00 a.m. until 3:00 p.m. each day, and in return I was given a small wage and anything left in the shop at the end of trade.

I continued to eat well, and I thoroughly enjoyed being active and productive again. In the afternoons I continued to work on restoring my new home.

I realised I was going to need some help, as I was clearly not qualified to build and thatch the roof, not to mention all the rest of the jobs that needed doing to make the place liveable. I was also on a tight budget as my wage was only small, and the money Mr. Baxter had given me was not going to last forever.

I asked around, and again my mother's God smiled upon me. It seemed that the more I was willing to help myself, the more support I was given.

Thomas, a local building apprentice, was working similar hours to mine and wanted all the extra experience he could get. He agreed to help me out a few hours each afternoon and again on weekends for a very reasonable rate. I jumped at the chance, and so began our partnership.

As well as being an excellent apprentice, he was also barely two years older than me, and ruggedly handsome. His smile sent chills through me, and his laugh lit up my world.

He was honest, kind, and playful, but never cruel or rude. We had fun together and grew closer as we spent more and more time in each other's company.

I was feeling more positive these days, and all the physical labour was doing my body a world of good. My new home was coming along well. I now had a completed roof and new windows and doors, as well as a working outdoor toilet and running water. The kitchen was almost usable, and for the first time in years, the home was almost habitable.

Chapter 21

One particularly hot day, after working in the afternoon sun for several hours, Thomas and I got into a water fight. It was fun and refreshing, and we both laughed as we chased each other around the farm. Luckily no one else was out in the heat of the day to see us acting like the children that, I suppose, we actually still were.

We sat down under the shade of the half-finished veranda and took a breather. "So," he said casually, "what did you do to your back?"

I hadn't realised I was wearing white, and my scars were visible under my water-soaked top. "Oh," I said cryptically, embarrassed and taken off guard, "I fought with a beast and paid the price, but I still won."

"I'll bet you did," he replied, his eyes filled with admiration and respect.

I told him the actual story.

He nodded sympathetically, and it felt good to actually talk about it.

"It's ugly though, isn't it?" I half-asked and half-stated.

"Nope," he replied genuinely. "It just makes you more intriguing. Anyway, I've got a few battle scars myself."

With that, he held out his hand and showed me a tiny scar on his index finger. It was barely visible and would have only been a centimetre long.

"Battle with a chicken," he stated proudly. "I was five at the time, so the chicken had an unfair advantage. If it tried it on now, I'm sure I could take it."

"Oh you poor battle-weary soldier," I said in jest. I asked as an afterthought, "What happened to the chicken?"

"Lunch."

We both laughed, as our stomachs growled. A chicken sandwich would be perfect.

Chapter 22

As I began to open my heart to Thomas, it became easier to trust others again. I spent time with the minister talking about my family history, and we compared memories. I was able to confide in him about the abuse, and it felt good to make sense of it with someone who was not judging me.

He validated my experiences and reaffirmed my strength and dignity as a person.

For the first time in many years I began to connect with others in the village, in particular, Thomas's three sisters, who welcomed me into their family home. Thomas had a mother *and* a father, and it was fascinating to see how a *real* family operated.

They argued and fought like normal people, but it was obvious they cared for each other and that his parents loved and respected each other.

At first I was jealous. I was angry and furious that they had the life I had missed out on, but as I talked this through with the minister, I realised I was being given a chance to connect with these people and experience what it was like to be welcomed. I could throw the opportunity away with bitterness and resentment, or I could accept the kindness and friendship they offered.

Thomas's family never treated me as though they pitied me, and I was grateful for this. Thomas and I would often have dinner with them when we had finished working, and I enjoyed sharing my goods from the bakery with them.

His sisters, all of whom were younger, loved to hear about my experiences in the abbey and in the orphanage, and they questioned whether God must be my dad. I assured them he wasn't, but they were not convinced. I still wasn't at the point of accepting that God loved me, but I was beginning to feel he was no longer rejecting me, and this felt good.

Sometimes Thomas's parents and sisters would come visit my new home, and they were genuinely impressed with the work we were doing. They were so proud of their son, and I got the distinct feeling they were proud of me too.

I discovered that by treating myself differently and by applying myself to something new, I didn't feel like that angry, poor, abused little girl anymore. I respected her and the experiences she'd had, and I was always willing to sit with her emotionally and show her love and compassion when that part of me was feeling vulnerable, but I also felt I had grown from those experiences, and that I was becoming a new, more well-rounded person. I began to develop a confidence in myself that maybe I too might have a decent future ahead.

Some nights Thomas and I camped out in the house together, sleeping on blankets on the floor. He never touched me or made any effort to get too close, but just sharing the space with him felt natural, comfortable, and intimate.

He was about to finish up his apprenticeship and was going to continue working for his boss at increased pay. Things were going well for him, and as I listened to him talk about plans for his future, I wondered where I fit within his life.

Chapter 23

Finally, after many months of hard yet enjoyable work, it was finished. My home was pretty much complete. The furniture was in, and a photo of my mother adorned the mantelpiece. My mother's family home had been restored from the ground up with love and respect, just as I had begun to do with myself. Sure I still had some work to do on a personal level, as we are always living, learning, and growing, but on the whole, I was satisfied. There was only one thing in my life that needed clarity.

As Thomas and I sat together on the comfy couch in front of the open fire, I stared into the flames to avoid his gaze. "So," I started. "I guess this is it, then," I stated with an air of finality in my voice.

"What's that then?" he asked.

"Well, tomorrow you are a free man, and I'm sure there will be other girls in the village who need homes built." I kept my gaze firmly on the flickering fire in front of me.

He was silent, but I felt his eyes boring into the side of my head. "Nah. They can find their own builders. I'm actually more interested in a much bigger project now. Maybe you could help me with it?"

His reply caught me off guard, and I looked at him with curiosity. He smiled like he was joking but his eyes were serious. He tried to keep his tone casual.

"Sure," I said, waiting for him to explain.

"Well, I was thinking, now we've finished building this house together, maybe it's time we started building a life together. That is, if you don't already have plans?"

Electricity coursed through my body and my hands began to shake. I tried to maintain my composure.

"That sounds good," I said as calmly as I could.

We smiled and then broke into laughter. He pulled me close and kissed me gently, and we melted into each other.

*   *   *

My name is Rose. My mother was a nun, but I am not, so I can choose a different life, and I think I may have just found my someone ...

About Rose

*R*ose: *My Mother Was a Nun* is the sequel to *Guided*. Rose's story picks up where we left her after the death of her mother.

This story touches on difficult and awkward subjects. It addresses the shadow side of life, the negative emotions and events that even in our very open society are still taboo.

The story addresses issues of bullying, sexual and physical abuse, abandonment, and suicide. The story provides the reader with enough information to work out what has happened without going into intimate details, so as not to overly traumatise the reader.

Rose's story needs to be heard because these are issues that are killing our children.

In society today, even without being in the situation Rose was in, many of us feel unheard, unseen, and abused. Whether this abuse is physical, sexual, or emotional, in some way we all have scars to remind us of the hardships of life.

Rose has her scars as a physical reminder of her pain, but many of us carry a pain that cannot be seen or known by others.

As we discovered in the first book 'Guided', Rose's mother had been fighting for survival against the soldiers. They were a real, objective threat. The whole country was aware of, acknowledging, and understandably concerned about the threat. The trauma of war was shared by everyone.

Rose's father had also fought for survival at a much more frontline level. The experience and the trauma destroyed his life. He was not able to process what had happened or share his experience. After the war, soldiers were just expected to suppress what they had seen and done and be "normal" around their loved ones. We can see how these experiences affected his ability to connect and ultimately led to him ending his life.

Though the circumstances were different, Rose, like her father, was fighting a silent war. She was isolated and bullied. She was being persecuted by her teacher and was being abused by Mr. Baxter. She was dealing with issues that no child should have to deal with and yet so many are.

Rose was clever and strong and resilient, but she still felt hopeless, out of control, and alone. Hers was a trauma that could not be shared and the consequences of disclosing these forms of abuse were too uncertain. In relation to bullying, she may have been disregarded or it may have made the bullying worse. Every child in the orphanage was probably experiencing a similar isolation and fear, but no one was able to share openly or honestly.

Similarly, with the abuse from Mr. Baxter, disclosing the abuse may have had consequences she couldn't control. She may have felt she only had one opportunity. Maybe she felt that if she told someone and wasn't believed that she would be punished. Adults tend to have a way of coping with things that include disregarding, actively denying, or rushing headfirst into a situation to fix the problem without consulting with or taking into account the needs of the person who has disclosed. These reactions can leave this person feeling even more helpless and out of control.

Rose's mother is an example of this. She was furious that Rose had been physically beaten, so her solution was to begin teaching at the school. Although this turned out to be a positive action, it left Rose feeling that she now had to protect herself and her mother, as well as manage her mother's emotional reaction to the abuse.

It is so important that the problem solving happens *with* the person who is experiencing the trauma. Sometimes just talking through the options helps the person feel he or she is being heard and validated and that the situation will be handled safely and calmly and that the process has been well thought out.

Responding rather than reacting is an important consideration.

In the story, Rose speaks about connection being more important than love. Potentially, this is because we all have an innate ability to love. We are all capable of love, yet we are also capable of causing great hurt to ourselves and those around us.

It is likely that many of the people in Rose's life, her birth father and mother, and even Mr. Baxter loved her, yet they still made choices that resulted in devastation and destruction for themselves and those around them. It was not a lack of love that damaged Rose, it was the expression of that love.

In many ways loving is easy, but connecting is hard. Connecting is the action point. It is the active expression of love. It is the way we speak or listen or seek to understand someone we care about. We all express our love differently, and we all have differing needs for connection from others.

How do you connect with others? How would you like others to connect with you?

In many ways, Mr. Baxter loved Rose. He gave her gifts and physical affection. He spoke kindly and gave her his time. When she fell pregnant he respected her enough not to put her through another termination, so he stayed away. In his eyes, he was behaving appropriately, and because Rose was not saying no and actively fighting him off, she was consenting to the relationship.

What he was not taking into account was that he was in a position of power over her, and she did not feel she had the free will to say no. She was isolated and unable to fully consent to the relationship. Her trust was violated by someone who, as an adult, should have known better. It is easy to see how confusing this must have been for a child in Rose's position.

These days we are afraid to face our shadow sides, and we are afraid to sit with others' shadows. We don't want to admit that difficult experiences are real, and we try to protect ourselves by denying their existence.

We are confused because life is not all good or bad, and people are not only good and evil. Sometimes the perpetrators of abuse are actually dealing with their own issues, and they do things that are unacceptable.

This is not to justify any sort of abuse, but it helps us understand why walking away or speaking out is not always the first response of those affected by abuse.

It is difficult when you know someone's actions are going to break your world apart. In Mrs. Baxter's case, for example, we do not know if she knew of the abuse, but when Rose says Mrs. Baxter's pain pills and sleeping pills did not help, we are led to ask why Mrs. Baxter would need these pills in the first place. We know Mrs. Baxter was unable to have children. Did she feel guilty that she could not give her husband an heir and therefore he was allowed to go elsewhere for physical connection? Did she keep quiet about the abuse so that she could have "girls of her own" in the home? Did she know that if she spoke out she would lose the empire they had built together? Or did she genuinely have no idea of what was going on?

These are the sorts of questions people suffering abuse might be asking, and people who have had these experiences are often accused of being paranoid, but it is possible they are just unable to trust because they have learnt no one will protect them.

Rose needed protection, but apart from her mother she had no one but herself to rely on. In 'Guided' we discovered that Rose's mother could talk to angels, her mother's mother had protected her from beyond the grave in visions to keep her safe, and her Mother Superior had given her protection and nurtured her talents. Rose did not have the benefit of these supports.

Rose's mother did all she could to protect her daughter. She began to teach at the school so Rose would not be beaten and bullied, but she was not able to protect her from what she experienced when she was not around.

Rose had to develop her own problem-solving abilities, and to her credit she felt she was handling these challenges quite well. Rose's mother felt eternally guilty for not being able to do more for her daughter, but at no point did Rose feel let down by her mother or hold her responsible for the events of her life. In fact, she prided herself on being self-sufficient.

In the story we know Rose was a bright girl who craved adventure. She was bored with the monotony of the abbey and her schoolwork. When the Beast punishes her for saying her times tables too fast, we can only imagine that Rose is far more intelligent than the Beast would like. We are led to wonder where Rose would have ended up if her education had been extended.

Although she put on a brave face, Rose, like all of us, still craves connection with a special someone, but she becomes angry when connection is offered, in the case of Thomas's sisters. Many times we surprise ourselves with our emotions. They come out unpredictably. Sometimes what we most desperately want we cannot accept because on some level we feel unworthy or are fearful that the connection will not last.

We are afraid to trust because we fear our needs will not be met or that the connection will fade away. We are longing for someone who will be there for us forever and become anxious when we think of losing that connection.

This is an inherent human characteristic whether we have experienced abuse or not.

When we have the belief that we are bound to get hurt and abused and that we cannot trust anyone, we ultimately seek to test the theory, often by constantly testing other people. We seek to push them away or force them to abandon us, just to prove a point. Our emotions get out of control, and we are torn between great love and great hate for those we wish we could get close to.

The trouble with attempting to connect in this actually quite logical way is that even the kindest, most genuine of people will eventually burn out and be unable to tolerate these mood swings.

So what is the alternative?

Rose developed a relationship with herself first. She got to know more about herself and how she responded to and lived her family history. She looked honestly at the things she was using to get her through the day and chose to slowly rebuild herself into a functional human being.

What we see in Rose is a strength of character and a resilience. She doesn't know what life holds for her, but she is willing to give it a go. She is willing to take responsibility for the course of her life. She takes charge of solving her own problems, and when she is faced with something she cannot manage alone she seeks help. Despite thinking her mother had rejected her when she did not respond to her letter, she speaks openly to her mother about this. She is not afraid to be open where she needs to be. Later she seeks help from the minister, and these help-seeking behaviours seem to have had a positive effect on her ability to cope and move forward in her life.

Rose discovered that she needed to choose life and began acting as though she intended to live. We as humans have a capacity to love and support and care, but we also have a capacity to get burnt out.

Rose handled this by containing her emotion where possible. She did not destroy the relationships with Thomas's sisters by showing them her fury. This was not their issue. It was hers. Instead she spoke to someone impartial whom she could trust.

She did not live with the minister or call him at all hours of the night, she consulted him with the intention of responsibly understanding her history and more of herself.

She connected well with Thomas, but again, she did not blurt out her history and drown him in it on their first meeting.

It takes time to get to know someone, and sometimes our histories need to be revealed slowly and appropriately.

Rose was looking only for her "someone," as though one other person could complete her, but this is a lot of pressure to place on someone, and it may be far more helpful to buffer yourself against the uncertainty of life by having realistic connections with more than one person, such as friendships, love relationships, family relationships, mentoring relationships, etc. In this way it is possible to experience a range of positive connections rather than pinning your hopes on only one person.

Rose feels quite emotionally disjointed at times. She is working at piecing her life together to better understand her family history. She only has access to limited information, and in the case of speaking to the minister about how he "saw" an apparition of her mother, Rose clearly doubts the accuracy of some of this history.

In our own way we are all trying to piece together our histories, whether this is as far back as a past life experience or a present one. We all long to feel as though we fit in or belong to something bigger than ourselves. Rose's plight illustrates how difficult it can be to understand the past, a feeling that may be shared by those who have been adopted, emigrated, or who have lost loved ones through death or separation.

All families have their stories. Some are talked about often and repeated ad nauseam, and some are skilfully hidden from family members as well as outsiders, due to issues of shame, fear of judgement, or anger.

What are some of your favourite family stories? What do you remember from when you were younger? Does your family hold any secrets? What would happen if these stories were shared?

Our stories make us who we are, and they are unique to us. Sometimes we can heal the past simply by changing the way we tell the story. When each person's perspective is taken into account and the story is understood in a different way, it leaves a person open to releasing the emotions that previously kept them stuck.

In our lives we all have experiences that are difficult, and we are transformed by these trials. It is how we choose to respond to these events that determine the quality of our lives.

Rose was perceived differently by her mother and her friends. In what ways do your family and friends see you differently to others who know you less well? If you had everyone you know in one place, could you still be yourself or would you need to cycle through different personalities?

How important is it to have a cohesive character?

Rose felt she was protecting her mother when her mother began to teach at the school. She took on an overwhelming responsibility in feeling she had to make things better for her, and when she heard her mother was sick, she believed it was her fault.

How would this have affected Rose on a physical or emotional level? Have you ever felt you were responsible for protecting someone? Is it fair to believe you could? Do you hold guilt about letting someone down? How have you managed these feelings? Are you still trying to make up for this with everyone else you come into contact with, or did the guilt cause you to shut down? If you did both, how difficult is it to manage these conflicting strategies?

Rose went to great lengths to protect herself from bullying. Some would argue that the physical pain and the scars that went with it were more than any bully would have inflicted, but it shows us the impact emotional bullying was having on her. Have you ever been bullied before? How did you manage it? Rose's attempts resulted in lifelong scars and an increase in status that still separated her emotionally from her peers. Was there anything else she could have done that would have been less painful?

Rose had several role models, all whom she loved and respected, but she chose to live her life her way. When she says, "My mother was a nun but I am not, so I can choose differently," she is acknowledging that it is okay to love someone but make different choices to what they would have made.

Where in your life have you had to step up and take responsibility for yourself? How did it feel? Where in your life do you need to do this now?

Rose's transformation took time. It is hard to face your shadow side, your past, and your emotional baggage. It's difficult to connect when you don't know how, but it is always possible.

When you are by yourself, how do you feel about yourself? How can you give yourself the time and attention you deserve? How can you be a better friend to yourself?

As Rose began to accept herself more, her perception of her relationship with God changed. Her mother connected to God when she was feeling vulnerable, whereas Rose began to connect with God more when she was stronger.

Do you have a personal connection with a higher power? Why or why not? During which circumstances do you connect with this power?

Rose's story shows us that life is what we make of it. It is not always smooth, but it is our life. When we are intent on making things better, opportunities come our way.

Having shared in Rose's story, how will you choose to understand the story of your own life, and how will you use your own personal transformation to make *your* life better?